The
MAGIC FOX

The
MAGIC FOX

By Paula Harrison

Illustrated by SOPHY WILLIAMS

ALADDIN

New York London Toronto Sydney New Delhi

For Sally, Poppy, and Florence

ALADDIN

An imprint of Simon & Schuster Children's Publishing Division

1230 Avenue of the Americas, New York, New York 10020

First Aladdin paperback edition November 2017

Text copyright © 2016 by Paula Harrison

Illustrations copyright © 2016 by Sophy Williams

Originally published in Great Britain in 2016 by Nosy Crow Ltd.

Published by arrangement with Nosy Crow

Also available in an Aladdin hardcover edition.

All rights reserved, including the right of reproduction in whole or in part in any form.

ALADDIN and related logo are registered trademarks of Simon & Schuster, Inc.

For information about special discounts for bulk purchases, please contact Simon & Schuster Special Sales at 1-866-506-1949 or business@simonandschuster.com.

The Simon & Schuster Speakers Bureau can bring authors to your live event. For more information or to book an event contact the Simon & Schuster Speakers Bureau at 1-866-248-3049 or visit our website at www.simonspeakers.com.

Cover designed by Steve Scott

Interior designed by Nina Simoneaux

The text of this book was set in ITC Clearface.

Manufactured in the United States of America 1017 OFF

2 4 6 8 10 9 7 5 3 1

Library of Congress Control Number 2017941297

ISBN 978-1-4814-7620-1 (hc)

ISBN 978-1-4814-7619-5 (pbk)

ISBN 978-1-4814-7621-8 (eBook)

Chapter One

* .:*

Poppy's Candles

Poppy skipped along the cobbled street carrying a large wicker basket. Her red hair was tied into two bunches that bounced on her shoulders with every skip. She was wearing a long yellow dress and a gray cloak that was tied tightly under her chin. The little town of Penlee was high up in the hills and the wind could be cold even in the summertime.

"Morning, Poppy!" Mr. Lott called from the bakery. "Have you sold many candles today?"

"Yes!" Poppy paused by the open doorway and breathed in the lovely smell of freshly baked bread. "I've completely sold out of Red Flamers. Lots of people have bought Blue Whispers too." She pulled back the green cloth that was covering her basket and showed him the rows of brightly colored candles inside. "Would you like anything?"

"One Golden Sparkle, please." Mr. Lott handed her a silver coin and a piece of cherry cake in a paper bag. "Here, take this! You must be hungry after all that walking."

"Thank you!" Poppy beamed, taking the bag and handing him a tall golden candle. Mr. Lott's cakes were the nicest in the whole of Penlee. "I'd better go back home and get some more candles. See you soon!"

Mr. Lott smiled. "Bye, Poppy! Take care!"

Poppy skipped down the lane, her gray cloak streaming out behind her. Before she went home, she would stop at the park, she decided. There was a group of scarlet foxes living in a den between the roots of a tree. She'd made friends with them a few weeks ago, and she loved to watch them playing together. She was sure they'd like a little piece of her cake.

The scarlet foxes were magical creatures. They had wise green eyes and their copper-red fur was even brighter than Poppy's hair. But the strangest thing was that each one had several tails. The younger ones had three while the biggest foxes had five. The old stories said that their magic came from their tails, but Poppy didn't know if that was true.

In a shimmer of magic, the scarlet foxes could change color to match their surroundings. A sudden noise would make them hide in the bushes. Then their coats would transform to green and brown, leaving them almost invisible among the leaves and branches. Poppy was astonished every time she saw it.

She smiled. What would she do if she could change color? Would she camouflage herself and turn invisible like the magical foxes? Or would she turn a bright color like her candles? She was so busy thinking about it that she bumped into a girl coming the other way along the street.

"Oh, Poppy!" snapped Natasha, flicking back

her dark hair. "Stop daydreaming! I'm sure my arm's bruised where you hit me with that basket of candles."

"Sorry, Natasha!" Poppy dodged round her and carried on down the street. Natasha was nine years old like Poppy, and she helped out in the shoemaker's shop. Poppy sometimes wondered why she always seemed so cross.

People smiled and nodded to Poppy as she ran past. She had sold candles in the town ever since her aunt and uncle had agreed that she was strong enough to carry the basket. Poppy's parents had died from a fever when she was a baby, and she had lived with her aunt and uncle ever since. Their little cottage stood on a hill near the edge of Penlee. From her bedroom window Poppy had a wonderful view of the river, which ran just outside the town.

Poppy's aunt and uncle were the only candle-makers in Penlee. They had a workshop in the garden behind their house, where they shaped the candles from warm wax and hung them up to dry.

They sold lots of different kinds of candles. There were Red Flamers that burned with a long red flame, and Blue Whispers whose flame was a beautiful soft blue. There were Golden Sparkles that gave out a fountain of glittering sparks and were perfect for birthday cakes! Sometimes her aunt would make amazing molds and shape the wax into elephants or castles or unicorns.

Poppy loved watching the candles being made. There was a cabinet filled with little bottles of powder that her aunt would pour into the soft wax before stirring it. She wasn't allowed to touch these special ingredients, but her aunt and uncle had promised her that one day they'd teach her what to do.

Weaving through the narrow streets, Poppy passed the shoemaker's and the tea shop. She was just about to turn another corner when she noticed a group of people gathered round a sign that was nailed to the church gate. Some were shaking their heads as they read it. Poppy moved closer to take a look. She read:

Magical animals are dangerous. Do not go near them or assist them in any way. Anyone disobeying this order will be punished.

By order of Sir Fitzroy, on behalf of Queen Viola, the ruler of the Kingdom of Arramia.

Poppy read it three times to make sure she hadn't made a mistake. Why did the sign say that magical animals were dangerous? The scarlet foxes would never hurt anyone! They were funny, clever creatures and they seemed very gentle.

There were all kinds of magical animals in the kingdom—including dragons, star wolves, and sky unicorns—but most were shy creatures and kept away from towns like Penlee. Poppy had never heard of a magical animal harming anybody.

"I've heard of that man, Sir Fitzroy," said Mrs. Allen, the flower seller. "He's a knight at the royal castle. People say that the queen believes everything he tells her."

"This sign is such nonsense!" replied Mr. Denton, the shoemaker. "And anyway, we hardly ever see magical creatures in Penlee."

Poppy hurried away, worry gnawing at her insides. Mr. Denton was right, but he didn't know about the magical scarlet foxes. They'd made their den in a corner of the park where they were hidden by trees and thick bushes. She didn't think anyone had noticed them except her.

Stopping at the park gate, Poppy looked round carefully before hurrying in. There was a huge willow tree in one corner, with long branches that hung right down to the ground. Poppy pushed apart the curtain of leaves and stepped inside. She felt safe here because the branches screened her from the rest of the park.

A whiskery nose poked out of a hole between the willow's roots, and a pair of green eyes watched Poppy curiously.

"Hello!" said Poppy softly. "Aren't you coming out to play?"

The fox's ears pricked up but he didn't come out of the hole.

Poppy set down her basket and took out the paper bag that held Mr. Lott's cherry cake. The bag rustled as she opened it, and the fox crept out of his den. Sniffing at the bag, he barked softly.

A cluster of foxes poured from the hole. Poppy counted five of them, but only two looked fully grown. "You must be a family," she murmured. "With two parents and three children."

The smaller ones scampered around, chasing one another. Poppy carefully broke five small pieces off the cherry cake and laid them on the grass. "It's a good thing Mr. Lott gave me such a large slice. There's still a little piece left for me too!"

The foxes nibbled at their cake and Poppy sat down to eat hers. The creatures looked hopefully at her when they finished. The smallest fox, which had fluffy red fur and three curly tails, crept up and put a paw on Poppy's knee.

"I'm sorry!" began Poppy. "I haven't got any more, but—"

A loud rumbling

drowned out the rest of her words as a cart came down the street behind the park. Instantly, the largest fox switched color to match the curtain of willow branches. The others all changed to match the grass. Poppy could barely make them out against the green background.

Only the littlest fox didn't change. She closed her eyes and went very still as if she was concentrating. Then one ear turned yellow to match Poppy's dress and one leg went green. The rest of her fur stayed as red as before.

The small creature opened her eyes and looked in surprise at her green leg.

Poppy giggled. "You're still learning! I think that's a very good try!"

The little fox gave a high bark as if she was pleased too. The bigger foxes gathered round and they all started to play again.

Poppy smiled at them all. She remembered the sign near the church: MAGICAL ANIMALS ARE DANGEROUS.

It was the silliest thing she'd ever heard!

Chapter Two

✦ ✶ ❋

The Children and
the Dragon

Poppy didn't want to say good-bye to the scarlet foxes, but she knew she had to get home and collect more candles to sell. She hurried up the hill toward her aunt and uncle's house.

The wind grew stronger and Poppy's cloak swirled around her legs. She glanced at the gray clouds sailing overhead. She hoped it wasn't going to rain. Pulling up the hood of her cloak, she noticed something in the sky that didn't look like a cloud at all—a shape with huge leathery wings.

A dragon.

Poppy's skin tingled. She'd never seen a dragon so close to Penlee before. It was black with a crest of red spines along its back. She held her breath as it wheeled round and flew south, beating its enormous wings.

A boy and a girl came running down the street. They stopped to wave at the sky.

"Thank you, Bellegar!" called the boy.

"See you soon!" shouted the girl.

The dragon gave a deep growl as it flew away.

Poppy stared at the children in astonishment. Why were they talking to the dragon? She knew they weren't from Penlee because she'd never seen them before. Neither of them had cloaks, and the girl wore a short green dress and sandals.

The boy noticed Poppy and nudged the girl.

"Hello!" called Poppy. "Do you know that dragon?"

"He's our friend," said the boy. "We wouldn't have got here without him."

"Really?" gasped Poppy. "You flew here?"

"It's true!" The girl gave Poppy a serious look. "We're friends of magical animals—ALL magical animals. Actually, that's why we're here. The magical creatures in this kingdom are in danger and we're trying to help them."

Poppy stared. First that horrible sign had

gone up on the church gate and now this girl and boy were talking about magical animals. It was all very strange. She had to find out more. "Would you like something to eat?" She pointed to her house. "I live just there, and my aunt makes really nice cookies."

The girl and boy exchanged looks.

"I think we should stop for a while," the boy said. "I'm hungry."

"All right, but we don't have long," said the girl. "Bellegar's gone to the river for a drink. After he's rested we'll need to fly on to meet our friend Sophy." She turned to Poppy. "Thanks for inviting us! I'm Talia and this is Lucas."

"I'm Poppy. Come inside and we can talk." Poppy led them up the front path. "My aunt and uncle won't interrupt us. They'll be busy making candles in the workshop."

She took them into a room decorated with candles of all shapes, sizes, and colors. Poppy's favorite were the purple butterflies on the mantelpiece, which had delicate wax wings. Talia and Lucas followed her, looking curiously at the wax sculptures.

Poppy led them into the kitchen and fetched some lemonade and the cookie tin. She longed to ask more about the dragon. "What is it like to fly?" she burst out. "It must be awesome!"

"It's wonderful!" said Talia. "You can see everything when you're up there in the sky—all the trees and rivers. We come from far away in the Hundred Valleys. I never dreamed I would get to see places like this!"

Poppy poured the lemonade and offered them chocolate cookies. "So why do you say that the magical animals are in danger? A sign has gone

up in the middle of town saying we should keep away from the creatures." She swallowed, thinking of the scarlet foxes. "It says we shouldn't go near them at all."

Talia set her cup down with a snap. "I bet that's Sir Fitzroy's fault! He's sending orders all around the kingdom to stop people from helping them."

Lucas watched Poppy closely. "Do you know any magical creatures? Are there any living in this town?"

Poppy hesitated, then decided she could trust

Talia and Lucas. "There are scarlet foxes." She told them about the foxes with their beautiful coats that transformed to any color. "And this Sir Fitzroy you mentioned—his name is on the sign I told you about."

"He's a knight at the royal castle," Talia told her. "I only found out about him when Sophy gave me my Speaking Stone. She works as a maid there."

"Your Speaking Stone?" Poppy looked confused.

Talia took a small purple bag from her pocket. "There isn't much time to explain. Sir Fitzroy and his friends hate the magical animals. They believe the creatures are dangerous and they want to capture them. A group of us—me, Lucas, Sophy, and others—are secretly helping the animals." She stopped and bit her lip. "If you wanted, you could help us too."

"Yes, please!" Poppy said eagerly. "I think magical animals are amazing."

"Let's see if there's a stone for her!" Lucas's eyes gleamed.

"That's what I'm doing!" Talia opened the bag and poured a handful of little stones onto the table. "Hold out your hand, Poppy. These stones are magical and maybe one of them can be yours."

Poppy held out her hand and Talia placed a rock on her palm. It was dull and gray, and felt rough against her skin. "Are they really magical?" she asked as Talia took away the stone and tried the next one. "They look so ordinary."

"Just wait!" said Lucas, leaning forward. "It could be the next one."

Poppy frowned. "But what's supposed to happen? I just don't—" She broke off as her hand tingled.

The stone grew warmer and warmer, as if a fire burned inside it. Slowly the rock brightened from gray to orange.

"This is your stone, Poppy," breathed Talia. "I was sure you'd have one!"

"But why is it so hot? Ouch!" Poppy dropped the stone on the table as it became too hot for her fingers.

"It's the magic working!" Talia told her.

Glowing a fierce orange, the stone suddenly snapped in half.

"Oh no, it's broken!" gasped Poppy. "Did I do something wrong?"

"That's supposed to happen," Lucas reassured her. "The enchantment is hidden inside the stone. When it reaches the right person it breaks open and the magic begins!"

"Really?" Poppy peered at the stone. Inside each half was a hollow filled with glittering crystals as white as mountain snow. "It's beautiful! Is it really mine?"

Talia nodded. "And you must keep it a secret. Wear it on a thread around your neck like Lucas and I do." She pulled out her own stone tied to a thin piece of cotton. "It's not just a pretty stone—it's useful, and it will help you protect magical animals."

"But how?" Poppy picked up the two halves of rock. As she turned them, the crystals sparkled in the light.

"Didn't we tell you?" Talia smiled. "That is your Speaking Stone. It will let you talk to magical animals!"

Chapter Three

* · ·*

The Blast of the Horn

Poppy picked up her enchanted stone and held it tight. Talia was explaining how the stones had been discovered at the royal castle when the queen, not realizing how special they were, threw them away.

Poppy tried to listen carefully but she could hardly sit still. This stone would let her talk to magical animals. That meant she could go back to the park and speak to the scarlet foxes. There were so many things she'd love to ask them!

"So we had to save the firebirds and that's how our adventure began," finished Talia. "I wish we could stay longer, but our dragon, Bellegar, will be waiting for us."

"Thank you for my Speaking Stone." Poppy smiled. "I'll use it to help magical creatures as much as I can."

"I know you'll do a great job!" Talia got up. "Come on, Lucas. You know Bellegar hates waiting."

"Are you going far?" asked Poppy.

"We're on our way to the castle to give the unopened stones back to Sophy," said Talia. "We were looking after them in case Sir Fitzroy got suspicious, but now she needs them back again."

"Take some of these with you," said Poppy, holding out the cookie tin.

"Thanks!" Lucas took a handful of cookies and shoved them in his pocket before following Talia out the door.

Poppy quickly dashed up to her bedroom. Her window looked out over the countryside. She saw Talia and Lucas rushing down the hill. In the distance a black dragon was waiting beside the river.

Opening her sewing box, Poppy cut a length of blue thread. She tied the two halves of her stone together and hung it round her neck. No one would see it there, tucked beneath her dress.

She smiled. Now she could go to find the scarlet foxes!

Poppy filled her basket with more candles before dashing back into town. Her aunt had made a batch of little elephants with lovely curved trunks in purple wax. She was sure lots of people would love them.

Before going to sell the candles, she crept back to the willow tree in the park. As soon as she pushed aside the curtain of leaves, the scarlet foxes came out of their den. The smallest cub

bounded over, sniffing at her hands. Then she gazed at Poppy hopefully.

"You're hoping there's more cake, aren't you?" said Poppy, smiling. "I'm sorry, I haven't got any more."

The foxes stared at her in surprise. Poppy glowed with happiness. She was sure they'd understood exactly what she'd said.

The little cub ran back to the biggest fox. "Daddy! The girl talked to me. She did! She did!"

"I heard her, Little-paw," said the larger fox.

Poppy realised she'd startled them. "I'm sorry! I didn't mean to surprise you." She set down her basket and took out her magical stone. "I was given this. It's called a Speaking Stone. The people who gave it to me said it would let me talk to magical animals, and it works!"

The large fox came closer and stared at the

glittering white crystals inside the stone. "I have heard of these Speaking Stones. When I was a cub, my grandfather told me about them. He met a human who owned one and they understood each other through the stone's enchantment. People and magical animals were more friendly toward each other in those days."

"As soon as I got it, I knew I had to come and see you. I wanted to speak to you properly for the very first time!" said Poppy shyly. "My name's Poppy. I love coming here and watching you play together."

The biggest fox bowed his head. "I am Long-shanks and this is my wife, Bright-fur." He turned to the smaller foxes.

"And these are our children: Quick-eye, Sleepy-tail, and Little-paw."

The smaller foxes bowed their heads. The littlest cub bounced on her paws. "You're Poppy! Like the flower?"

"Yes, just like the flower." Poppy knelt down and stroked her warm fur. "It's lovely to talk to you, Little-paw."

She was about to ask them whether they liked living in Penlee when she heard a horn blowing loudly.

"What's that?" said Little-paw, trembling.

"I don't know." Poppy frowned. "It might be something important. I'd better go and see." She patted the little cub before gathering up her basket.

The horn blast came again.

"That could mean danger!" said Bright-fur, her five tails swishing.

"Everyone back to the den!" barked Long-shanks. "Quickly now!"

The fox cubs bolted into the hole, followed by their parents. Poppy watched them disappear into the darkness. She would have liked to talk to them for longer, but the noise of the horn had frightened them.

Poppy left the park and crossed the cobbled street. People were pouring from their houses and hurrying toward the center of town.

"Freshly made candles!" she called to them. "Pretty candles!"

"There's no time for that, Poppy!" Mr. Lott from the bakery dashed past. "That horn means some kind of emergency."

The horn blasted for a third time. Turning the corner, Poppy could see everyone gathering by the church gate. A knight was standing there in glistening silver armor. He was flanked by four guards. One of them was holding the horn.

Natasha elbowed past her. "Mind out, Poppy! Having those candles doesn't make you more important, you know."

Poppy sighed. Why did Natasha always have to be so rude? Holding her basket carefully, she slipped through the crowd to get closer to the front. She stood on tiptoes to try to see over the heads of all the people.

"Silence! We must begin." The knight stared down his long nose at the people gathered

around him. "My name is Sir Fitzroy and I am the queen's most important knight."

Poppy's mind whirled. Sir Fitzroy! That was the name she'd read on the sign—the same knight that Talia and Lucas had talked about.

"I'm here on behalf of Queen Viola, ruler of our kingdom," continued Sir Fitzroy. "There are evil powers in this land. There are things that would seek to harm the queen herself!"

Poppy's eyes widened. This really *was* an emergency then. Who would want to hurt the queen?

The crowd started talking but they fell silent again under Sir Fitzroy's dark glare.

"I'm talking about these wicked magical animals, of course!" the knight went on. "They have a dangerous power, and we can no longer allow them to roam freely in our land. From this moment, anyone who sees one of the creatures *must* report it to a guard. Then we will capture the beast and take it away."

Poppy's insides filled with fluttering panic. Talia and Lucas had been right. Sir Fitzroy wanted to capture all the magical animals. She couldn't let that happen to the scarlet foxes!

Chapter Four

✦ ∴ ✳

The Horrible Machine

Poppy stared at Sir Fitzroy as he carried on talking. She ought to go and warn the foxes about him straightaway. Then they could escape from town when night fell. Once they'd reached the countryside there would be lots of places for them to hide.

She began edging toward the back of the crowd, trying not to bump anyone with her basket. Sir Fitzroy went on talking about all the magical animals he wanted to catch.

Poppy crept past Mr. Lott, who was muttering, "Whoever heard of a dangerous sky unicorn or a deadly star wolf? This is ridiculous!"

"And if anyone disagrees with these orders, my guards will march them to the castle where they can explain their disloyalty to the queen!" yelled Sir Fitzroy.

Mr. Lott gulped and fell silent.

Poppy reached the back of the crowd. She glanced at the empty street behind her. All she had to do was sneak away without anyone noticing. Pulling up her gray hood, she edged away from the crowd.

"To make everything quicker, I have invented this magical-animal detector." Sir Fitzroy held up a large wooden box. "Inside here is a machine that can detect any magical beast close by, even if they're hiding in a hole or up a tree. It will make catching the disgusting creatures *much* simpler!"

Poppy's stomach gave a horrible lurch. If Sir Fitzroy's machine worked, then the foxes weren't even safe in their den till nighttime.

Sir Fitzroy set the box down and ordered two of the guards to lift out the machine. Two metal cogwheels stood on the wooden casing. One was much larger than the other. A handle was attached to the smaller wheel. A thick metal chain ran round the larger cogwheel and was linked to a metal spike that pointed straight upward. The spike had a sharp arrow shape jutting from the side.

Poppy stared, unable to take her eyes off the horrible machine. Sir Fitzroy grasped the handle and pushed it round and round. The smaller cogwheel turned, pushing the bigger one. The metal chain began to move, spinning the nasty-looking spike. Slowly, the arrow fixed to the spike went round. A harsh whirring began that made Poppy's head ache. A few people clapped their hands over their ears.

"It works like this," Sir Fitzroy yelled over the noise. "The spike makes a vibration that matches the creatures' magic. Then the arrow points to where the beasts are hiding."

Poppy watched in horror as the arrow shuddered to a stop. It pointed down the street in the direction of the park.

"Aha!" shouted Sir Fitzroy. "So you do have a magical creature somewhere in your town. The machine has detected the beast already!"

Everyone in the crowd started talking at once. Poppy turned and raced down the street. Her breath caught in her throat as she ran. Throwing open the park gate, she dashed straight to the willow tree and ducked underneath the dangling branches.

"Long-shanks! Little-paw!" she panted, kneeling by the foxes' hole. "You're in terrible danger! You have to leave town right now."

Long-shanks's face appeared at the opening to the den. "What's going on? Is there a fire?"

Poppy swallowed. "No, there are some bad people who don't like magical animals. They'll capture you if you stay here. Please—you have to go!"

Long-shanks sprang out of the den, followed by Bright-fur and the three cubs. Little-paw was shivering with fright and her three tails drooped.

"But we can stay here," said Long-shanks. "They'll never find us in our den."

"They will!" said Poppy urgently. "The man in charge has a special machine that hunts down magical creatures. He'll find you even if you stay in the den. Turning invisible won't keep you safe either."

"She means to help us, my love," Bright-fur said to Long-shanks. "I think we should follow her advice. We can go to the river. There are many holes in the sandy riverbank that would make a good den."

"Let us go then!" Long-shanks called to the cubs. "Come, children—we're leaving! You must be ready to camouflage as soon as I tell you to."

Bright-fur bowed her head to Poppy. "Thank you, Poppy—friend of magical animals!"

"Good-bye!" Poppy watched the scarlet foxes dash out of the park in a flurry of tails. They scampered up the street toward the edge of town.

Just as they disappeared into the distance, Poppy's heart sank. There were four foxes running in a pack. One of the cubs was missing.

Poppy looked around. Where was the missing cub? And what if it was Little-paw?

A snuffling noise came from deep inside the den.

Poppy crouched down. "Little-paw?" she whispered. "Are you down there? Please come out!"

The cub gave a tiny whimper. "I can't come out. It's too scary!"

"Please, Little-paw!" She tried to think of something that would help. "If you do, I'll find you more cake."

A small black nose and a pair of green eyes

appeared at the opening to the den. "Really? More cake?"

"Definitely more cake!" agreed Poppy. "Come on, Little-paw! The others have gone. We have to get you out of here."

Little-paw scampered out of the den and jumped into Poppy's arms. Poppy held the cub tight. Little-paw's fur felt warm against her cheek.

"You know you're not supposed to be making friends with those creatures," said a voice behind Poppy. "You could be in big trouble."

Poppy leaped to her feet, holding on to Little-paw. Natasha was standing behind them, her arms folded.

"Natasha! You made me jump," said Poppy.

"You could be in *really* big trouble," repeated Natasha.

"Please don't tell!" pleaded Poppy. "Look at

her! You can see she's not dangerous. She's just a baby."

"But I'm growing quite big now," Little-paw piped up. "I'll grow even taller after some cake."

Poppy stroked the cub's ears. She knew that Natasha couldn't understand what Little-paw was saying. She had to make the other girl realise how important it was to help the little fox!

"That knight has orders from the queen and he says all magical creatures are dangerous." Natasha nodded her head as if that settled everything.

"It's not true!" Poppy

burst out. "Please don't tell anyone about this cub, Natasha. Her family have left town and I'm going to take her to join them. They'd never hurt anybody!"

The park gate creaked open and Natasha peeped through the willow branches. "The guards are here," she said shortly. "It's too late to take her anywhere now."

Poppy's heart pounded. "Little-paw, can you change color to match my cloak?"

Little-paw closed her eyes and screwed up her little black nose. Her body turned gray and became invisible against Poppy's cloak, but her head stayed bright red.

Natasha's eyes widened. "I've never seen them do that before!"

Poppy bit her lip. It looked as if the cub's head was floating beside her shoulder. It was clear that Little-paw's magic wouldn't keep her safe from the guards.

Little-paw opened her eyes. "How's that?"

"It's not quite right but don't worry," Poppy told her. "I'm going to find you somewhere to hide. You mustn't make a sound. Do you understand?"

"Yes, Poppy." The cub's body reappeared and her whiskers trembled. "Am I in trouble?"

"I'll look after you." Poppy kissed the cub's furry head and set her down on the ground. If she took the candles out of her basket maybe she could hide Little-paw in there. Then she could get past the guards without them spotting the cub. She hurriedly emptied the candles onto the grass.

"What are you doing?" hissed Natasha. "All your candles will get dirty."

"But this is an emergency!" Poppy dropped the last candle onto the ground. She was just about to put Little-paw into the basket when a guard pushed aside the willow leaves.

"What are you two doing?" he asked gruffly.

Poppy froze. She knew at any moment he'd look down and see Little-paw sniffing at the pile of candles. She had to think of something fast!

Chapter Five

✦ ∴ ✦

Natasha's Idea

Poppy took a step toward the guard. She had to keep his attention fixed on her so that he didn't notice Little-paw. She waved wildly with both arms. "Hello! Isn't it a nice day? We just wanted some shade under this tree."

At the exact same moment Natasha pulled off her cloak and threw it over the fox cub. Little-paw gave a tiny squeak and stopped moving.

The guard's eyes narrowed. "You're up to something, aren't you? I can spot a guilty face, you know."

"We were just resting." Poppy didn't dare look at Natasha's cloak in case the guard noticed. She longed for him to go away so that she could pick up Little-paw.

"There's a magical animal here," said Natasha shortly.

Poppy's shoulders drooped. How could Natasha give the cub away? And why did she bother hiding Little-paw under her cloak? It made no sense!

"What's that?" Sir Fitzroy burst through the

willow branches, his armor clanking. "Have you found one of the beasts? I knew the detector wouldn't let us down. Come here, Tepp! Bring the machine!"

A second guard stumbled in carrying the magical-animal detector. The two cogwheels turned and the metal spike spun slowly. Poppy swallowed, watching the arrow go round and round.

"Come *on*, Tepp! Where is the little beast?" said Sir Fitzroy impatiently.

The arrow trembled, pointing toward Natasha's cloak. Then it moved on to face the park gate.

"The arrow's leading us back to the street, sir," said the guard.

"First you said it was leading us into the park. Make up your mind, soldier!" snapped Sir

Fitzroy. "You're being almost as annoying as the stupid people of this town."

Natasha's eyes narrowed as she looked at Sir Fitzroy.

"It . . . um . . . I don't know." The guard moved the machine this way and that. The detector whirred fiercely. The arrow swung round but kept pointing toward the gate.

"I really think there's nothing here to catch, sir," said the guard at last.

"Nonsense!" Sir Fitzroy turned to the girls. "Which of you said that there was a beast here?"

"Me, sir! But I meant there *was* a magical animal," explained Natasha. "It ran away as soon as we got here. It went that way!" She pointed toward the center of town.

Poppy gave Natasha a grateful look. She'd protected Little-paw after all!

Sir Fitzroy gave a deep groan. "You were too slow again!" He snapped at the guards. "Get that machine working and pick up the trail, and you girls need to get out of here. We have work to do!"

Poppy's hands shook as she piled the candles back into her basket. Natasha gathered up her cloak, hiding the cub among the folds. Poppy held her breath, hoping that Little-paw wouldn't make a sound.

Sir Fitzroy turned away to give orders to the guards. Poppy and Natasha hurried out of the park and climbed the hill together.

"Let's go to my house," Poppy whispered to the other girl.

She didn't dare look back. Gradually her heart stopped beating so hard and she slipped Natasha a sideways glance. "Thanks for not giving Little-paw away! I really thought you meant to tell them at first. Why did you decide not to say anything?"

Natasha stuck her nose in the air. "I think magical animals should be protected. Anyway, I don't like that man very much!"

This was so different to what she'd said before that Poppy couldn't help giggling. Little-paw began to wriggle. "Where are we going, Poppy?" she called from under Natasha's cloak.

"We're going to my house," whispered Poppy. "Keep still, Little-paw! You can't come out until we've got inside."

"Why do you call her that?" Natasha asked curiously. "And why do you act like she can understand what you're saying?"

"Come inside and I'll explain. My aunt and uncle won't be back yet." Poppy ran to her front door and hurried inside.

Natasha stared wide-eyed at the magnificent candle sculptures in the living room. "Those are amazing!"

"My aunt made those butterfly ones," said Poppy. "I can give you one if you want."

"Yes, please!" Natasha flushed. Little-paw began wriggling under her cloak again. "I think I'd better set this cub free."

"Come in here!" Poppy beckoned Natasha into the kitchen. "We can't stay here long though! The guards could follow Little-paw's trail using that horrible detector."

Natasha set the cub on the ground and gently unwound her cloak from Little-paw's legs and tails. "There you are!" She turned to Poppy. "Getting out of town without someone spotting her will be much too hard! It's market day so lots of people are here. Someone's bound to see her. I think we should wait till nighttime and sneak her away in the dark." Her eyes gleamed with excitement.

Little-paw scampered across the kitchen floor, pounced on a tea towel and ran off with it in her mouth. Poppy smiled. It was nice to see her enjoying herself.

"What do you think?" said Natasha eagerly.

Poppy studied the other girl. Natasha really seemed to want to help. "So you really want to help Little-paw escape?" she asked Natasha. "It's just that . . . you never seemed to want to be friends before."

Natasha looked awkward. "You were always so busy selling your beautiful candles while I was stuck at the shoemaker's shop. I do want to help! This cub is so adorable and I don't like that nasty knight!"

Poppy smiled. "Neither do I! Well, it'll be easier with two of us keeping Little-paw safe."

"Why do you call her that?" Natasha asked again. "I'm sure there's something you're not telling me."

Poppy hesitated. Talia had advised her to keep her Speaking Stone a secret, but Natasha had helped save Little-paw. If they were going to finish this rescue together she ought to know everything. So she took out the stone and told Natasha all that had happened that morning.

Natasha listened closely. She was a little disappointed that the magic in the stone wouldn't work for her too, but she cheered up when Poppy got out some chocolate cake her aunt had made.

Little-paw seemed to like the cake too, and her red fur got covered in chocolatey crumbs. "This cake is even nicer than the last one!" she barked.

"So let's meet by the crossroads at midnight," decided Natasha. "Then we can sneak out of town."

"We can pretend we're gathering the night flowers that my aunt uses for some of her candles," said Poppy. "I'll bring my basket."

"Thanks for the cake!" Natasha knelt down and hugged Little-paw.

Poppy noticed how gentle she was with the fox cub. "Bye! See you at midnight!" She watched from the front window as the other girl made her way down the path. She remembered how Natasha's quick thinking had saved the cub from Sir Fitzroy. "It's been a day full of surprises," she told Little-paw. "And the biggest one has been Natasha!"

Chapter Six

✦ ⁖ ✦

Waiting for Midnight

Poppy took Little-paw upstairs. Her aunt and uncle would come back from the workshop soon and she didn't want them to find the fox cub in their kitchen. She knew they'd love Little-paw just as much as she did, but it didn't seem fair to get them into trouble with Sir Fitzroy.

The sun began to set. Little-paw fell asleep on Poppy's bed with her tails curled around her. Poppy went downstairs to have dinner.

"Are you all right, my dear?" said her aunt as she served the chicken pie. "You're very quiet."

"She's tired from selling all those candles, I expect," said her uncle.

"I'm fine!" Poppy smiled. "This pie is delicious. Could I have another piece?" When her aunt and uncle weren't looking, she carefully wrapped the extra pie in her handkerchief to take upstairs to Little-paw.

After eating the pie, Little-paw gazed out Poppy's window. "Is that shiny thing the river?

Is that where my mummy, daddy, Quick-eye, and Sleepy-tail have gone?"

"Yes, that's right." Poppy sat beside her. The river looked like a shining blue ribbon catching the last rays of the setting sun. "Soon you'll be there with them. We'll wait till it's dark and quiet and then I'll take you away from here."

Little-paw's nose quivered. "I liked it in our old den. It smelled like home!"

"I'm sure the new home your mummy and daddy have chosen is nice too," said Poppy, tickling her under the chin.

Little-paw climbed on Poppy's lap and fell asleep again. As she dreamed, parts of her changed color. One tail went leafy green, then her feet turned white and one ear went blue like the river. Poppy stroked her fur. She hoped the little cub was dreaming about something nice.

Poppy tried not to close her eyes. She was worried that if she went to sleep she wouldn't wake to meet Natasha at midnight. She read a story to herself. Then Little-paw woke up and she read a book to her. The story was all about a crafty fox who tricked a mean lion.

Little-paw got quite excited and made her read it three times. "I love it, Poppy!" She bounced on the bed, her tails swishing. "Especially the part where the fox scares the lion and eats all the pie!"

"That is a good bit!" Poppy noticed the time on her clock. "Oh, it's five minutes to midnight. We need to go!" She put on her cloak and shoes before showing Little-paw the basket. "Hop in here, Little-paw."

The cub jumped into the basket and Poppy laid a green cloth over the top.

"You need to stay in here until we've left town," she whispered. "No one must see you."

"It's bumpy in here!" said Little-paw fretfully. "I don't like it."

"It won't be for long." Poppy stroked the cub's ears gently. "We'll be down at the river soon."

Closing her door quietly, she tiptoed down the stairs. Her aunt and uncle had turned out the lamps and gone to bed long ago, but the fire in the hearth was still burning. Poppy took the lantern that hung on a hook by the door. She lit a candle from the fire and put it inside the lantern, closing the glass hatch firmly.

Bong! The church clock began to chime midnight. Natasha would be waiting!

Poppy slipped out the door into the darkness as the clock went on chiming. She held the basket carefully, keeping Little-paw steady. She was glad to find the streets completely empty. She needed to act as if she was going to gather night flowers, just in case someone came along.

She rounded a corner and caught a sudden movement. A black cat turned its bright-yellow eyes toward her before slinking away. Poppy carried on toward the crossroads.

A figure with a lantern stepped out of the shadows. "Hurry up!" hissed Natasha. "I've been waiting for ages."

"Did anyone see you walking here?" asked Poppy, glancing round nervously.

"No one at all!" Natasha reached into the basket and scratched Little-paw behind the ears. "Everyone's asleep."

The girls followed the road out of Penlee. As they passed the last house, they turned onto a smaller track that wound down the valley toward the river. A sprinkling of tiny stars glistened in the black sky.

Poppy and Natasha held their lanterns out in front of them and carefully picked their way down the stony path. As they passed a clump of bushes, Poppy caught sight of the river at the bottom of the slope.

"Who's there?" someone growled.

Natasha jumped and grabbed Poppy's arm, almost making her drop the basket.

One of Sir Fitzroy's guards peered at them in the lantern light. "Hey! Aren't you the girl with all the candles? What are you doing out here in the middle of the night?"

Poppy's hand shook and her lantern wobbled. "Sometimes I come out to pick the night flowers that grow by the river," she told him. "They're used for our Purple Dream candles that help people sleep. You can only pick them in the middle of the night otherwise their scent is lost." She didn't add that her aunt and uncle

were usually the ones who picked the flowers.

"And I came to help her," added Natasha.

The guard's face twisted suspiciously. "So what's in that basket then?"

"Nothing!" Poppy took a step back. "I haven't picked any of the flowers yet."

"Why is it bulging then?" The guard pointed

to the wrinkled cloth. Before Poppy could stop him, he snatched the cloth off the basket and peered inside.

There was nothing there.

Poppy's eyes widened. Where had Little-paw gone? Then she noticed a tiny movement at the bottom of the basket.

The guard tossed the cloth back on. "Hurry up and get your flowers then, but don't get in anyone's way."

"We won't!" Natasha pulled Poppy's arm.

Poppy longed to look in the basket again, but glancing back she saw the guard was still watching them. As soon as the path curved behind some trees, she stopped. "Little-paw?" she whispered, lifting the cloth. "Are you there?"

Something shifted inside—something that was exactly the same brown color as the basket itself. Three little tails flicked from side to side.

"I'm still here," said the cub. "I changed color all over!"

"You did it!" Poppy beamed. "Well done, Little-paw! That was just in time too."

"Shh! You'll make that guard come down here," Natasha warned Poppy before smiling down at the basket. "She's such a clever thing! I'd never have spotted her if I wasn't looking closely."

Little-paw's red ears appeared first, which looked very strange. Gradually the rest of her changed from brown to red too. "I closed my eyes and wished really hard," she said solemnly.

"You learned how to use your magic," said Poppy. "I bet your family will be just as proud as we are!"

Chapter Seven

* ·*

The Riverbank Den

Holding their lanterns high, Poppy and Natasha carried on down the slope to the river. Little-paw wanted to walk the rest of the way.

As there was no one in sight, Poppy decided it was perfectly safe.

On the riverbank, Natasha spotted some purple night flowers. "We should pick some. Then if we meet anyone else our story will seem more real."

A breath of wind rocked the flowers, making their sweet scent rise into the air. The girls knelt down and gathered several handfuls for Poppy's basket.

"I can smell them!" Little-paw danced round, flicking her tails.

"They smell lovely, don't they." Poppy lifted the flowers to her nose.

"No! Not the flowers!" Little-paw sprang away down the bank. "My family are here."

"Wait, Little-paw! We have to be careful," said Poppy, but the little fox had already vanished.

"Where did she go?" Natasha looked all around. The lantern cast warm light over the sandy bank and the dark, flowing river. "I hope she hasn't changed color again or we might never find her."

"Maybe she went in there." Poppy pointed to a row of holes in the bank. "Scarlet foxes are supposed to have a really good sense of smell. She'd know the right hole straightaway."

Little-paw's face appeared at the farthest hole. "My family were here—I know they were! But now they've gone. Why did they go away?"

"Maybe they just went to find some food," suggested Poppy. "I'm sure they'll be back soon."

Natasha blew out her lantern. "Put out your candle, Poppy! There are people down there."

Poppy saw lights moving near the bridge and quickly blew out her lantern. "I didn't see them before," she whispered. "They must have been hidden by those trees as we came down the track."

"There are at least four lanterns," said Natasha. "Who would come down here at night? I think we should find out what they're up to."

Poppy pulled a face. She thought they should stick to finding Little-paw's family, but before she could say so, the fox cub darted away again. "Little-paw, don't run off!"

The girls raced after her and found the cub hiding behind a huge rock close to the bridge. Poppy crouched down, putting an arm round Little-paw. "We have to stay together, okay?"

Little-paw pressed against her side. "All right, Poppy. I'll stay close to you."

Poppy peeked over the top of the boulder and her heart dropped like a stone. Four men stood round a large metal cage. Sir Fitzroy was leaning down, looking through the bars. Inside the cage were four scarlet foxes—Long-shanks, Bright-fur, and the other two cubs.

Poppy wasn't close enough to tell what the knight was saying, but she could hear the men laughing. Sir Fitzroy held the magical-animal detector up high and its arrow gleamed in the lantern light.

"We're too late," she whispered. "They must have used the machine to follow the foxes' trail out of town."

"I want my mummy and daddy!" whined Little-paw, and Poppy held her tight.

"We have to get the foxes out of there." Natasha bit her lip. "If we can get the guards away from the cage, then we can sneak over and set them free."

"They'll never leave the cage alone. I bet they'll load it onto a cart and take the foxes back to town to show everyone." Poppy rubbed her forehead. "The only thing that'd get their attention is another magical animal. Maybe that's it! We could get them away from the cage by showing them another magical creature."

Natasha's eyes widened. "Not this little cub? She could get caught."

"No, not Little-paw!" Poppy stroked the cub. "It shouldn't be a real magical creature at all. We can make one up!"

"Do you think that will work?" said Natasha doubtfully. "What creature should it be?"

Poppy thought hard for a moment. "How about a dragon? I can fetch a Red Flamer candle. It has a glowing flame that looks just like dragon's breath. We just need a way to get the candle into the air." Poppy frowned.

Natasha bit her lip. "It has to be really convincing otherwise the guards will never fall for the trick."

"They'll definitely notice the candle," said Poppy. "Red Flamers always look so bright in the dark."

"I've got an idea!" Natasha's eyes lit up. "I have a dragon kite at home. It's red and orange, and there are spines all the way down its back. In the daytime you'd know it was a kite straightaway but in the dark it might just trick them!"

"Brilliant!" Poppy's heart thumped faster. "Maybe if I tie my lantern to a long stick then I can get the candle flame high into the air too."

"We'd better fetch everything quickly." Natasha glanced at the guards. "Sir Fitzroy might move the foxes into town soon."

Poppy set the basket down behind the rock. She knew she'd be faster with less to carry. "Little-paw, we've got to fetch some things so we can rescue your family. Can you run?"

"I can run fast!" The cub leapt to her feet.

The girls dashed up the slope with Little-paw running on ahead. Once they reached Penlee,

Poppy tucked the cub under her cloak in case they met anyone on the street. First they went to Natasha's house and fetched the dragon kite from her shed. The brightly colored material and scary dragon eyes made the kite look fierce in the lantern light.

Hurrying down the street, Poppy led Natasha and Little-paw to her aunt and uncle's workshop. Taking the key from under the mat, she unlocked the door and went inside.

Natasha looked around in wonder as Poppy lit the lamp. "It's amazing in here!" She crossed the wooden floor, gazing at the tubs where the wax was heated. There were strings of multicolored candles hanging from the rafters.

Poppy picked up a Red Flamer candle and a long taper for lighting it. As candlemakers, her aunt and uncle had taught her how to light candles safely.

"How do those Red Flamer candles glow with such a bright-red color?" asked Natasha.

"My aunt and uncle use special ingredients like chili powder," Poppy told her. "Can you find me a long stick from the garden?"

Natasha dashed outside and came back a minute later with a long, straight branch. "I found this at the bottom of your garden."

While Natasha stripped the leaves off the branch, Poppy looped string through the handle of the lantern and tied it to the end of the stick.

Natasha smiled widely. "I think we're ready!"

Poppy picked up Little-paw and hugged her. "Let's try out this made-up dragon. I hope it gives that horrible Sir Fitzroy a fright!"

Chapter Eight

✦ ∴ ✸

The Flight of the Candle Dragon

When Poppy and Natasha got back to the river, the guards had begun loading the cage containing the scarlet foxes onto a cart. Sir Fitzroy was joking loudly that the foxes' magical invisibility could not defeat his amazing detector machine.

"Stay here until the men start chasing us," Poppy whispered to Little-paw. "Then go to your family and tell them we're going to set them free."

Natasha held the kite ready while Poppy used a taper to light the Red Flamer. She lifted the long stick into the air with the lantern tied to one end.

The Red Flamer lit up the night with a bright-red glow. Quickly, Natasha threw the dragon kite into the air and worked the strings. Once it unfurled, the kite looked nearly as big as a real dragon. The girls gazed upward. They had to keep the lantern and the kite close together to make the dragon trick work.

Swooping high, the dragon's tail fluttered

from side to side. The creature's black eyes shone as they caught the glow of the candle. Its fierce jaw hung open, filled with pointed teeth. Natasha hurriedly tugged the left string as the kite blew sideways in the breeze. Poppy lifted the lantern higher.

There was a shout from farther down the riverbank.

"A dragon!" yelled one of the guards.

"It's breathing fire!" called another.

"Catch that beast!" bellowed Sir Fitzroy. "I want that dragon."

"They've fallen for it!" gasped Natasha.

"I know!" cried Poppy. "Run!"

The girls raced down the riverbank. Poppy went first, leading the way with her Red Flamer. Natasha followed so that a dragon with a spiky tail streamed out behind the lantern.

Poppy's chest felt tight and her heart pounded. She could hear the men running. They mustn't let the guards catch up with them!

"Poppy!" gasped Natasha. "Put the candle out now. That way we're harder to find."

Poppy brought the branch down and quickly blew out the flame. Natasha ran on, pulling the kite behind her.

The men shouted to one another. They sounded closer.

Poppy's foot caught on a bramble but she managed to keep her balance.

"Throw the ropes!" bellowed Sir Fitzroy. "Catch the beast!"

Loops of rope came snaking through the air but they missed the girls completely. Poppy dashed round a bend in the riverbank and nearly ran straight into Natasha.

"I'll carry on!" gasped the other girl. "You go back and free the foxes."

"Are you sure?" panted Poppy.

"I'll keep them chasing the dragon kite for as long as I can," said Natasha. "Go!"

Poppy watched while Natasha sprinted away, the dragon flying high in the air behind her. Poppy ducked beside some water rushes as the guards chased after her friend. A minute later Sir Fitzroy stumbled after them.

When she was sure they were gone, Poppy crept out of her hiding place and stole back to the bridge. Little-paw was waiting by the cage. The cub put her front paws against the metal bars and whined.

"Stay calm, dear," said Bright-fur. "Here's Poppy now."

Poppy reached for the bolt high up on the cage door. The catch was stiff and it wouldn't move. She took hold of it with both hands. At last it slid back and Poppy swung the door open. Quick-eye and Sleepy-tail bounded out first, followed by their parents.

Bright-fur nuzzled Little-paw's face. "I was so worried about you, little one. We tried to go back and look for you, but then those men came."

"Thank you, Poppy," said Long-shanks. "You've helped us so much."

"What's this, Daddy?" Quick-eye nosed at a box on the ground. Inside were two cogwheels, a chain and a sharp metal spike.

It was the magical-animal detector.

"Keep away from it!" barked Long-shanks. "It's a wicked, nasty thing!"

Quick-eye jumped back and his ears flattened in alarm.

Poppy crept up to the machine. It had started whirring as it picked up on the foxes' magic. What should she do with it? She couldn't let Sir Fitzroy use it again, but she didn't really want to touch it. Shuddering, she managed to lift it up. Then she stumbled to the river's edge and threw it in.

The machine tumbled through the air. It gave a huge splash as it hit the water before sinking below the surface.

Little-paw gave a whoop and jumped round and round in a circle. "Splosh goes the machine! Poppy saves the day!"

Poppy grinned. It was lovely to see Little-paw so happy again.

"We must hurry. Those men may return soon."
Long-shanks began rounding up the cubs.

"Where will you go?" asked Poppy.

"I have cousins that live on the other side of
the green marsh. It's a swampy track and one
that humans seldom use. I think we will be safe
there." Long-shanks bowed his head. "Farewell,
Poppy. We will always remember your kindness."

"Good-bye and good luck!" Poppy bowed
to each fox in turn and then gave Little-paw a
big hug. The cub rubbed her
nose against Poppy's neck. She
stroked Little-paw's ears.
"I'll never forget you,
Little-paw!"

The scarlet foxes
scampered over
the bridge with

Long-shanks leading the way. As they reached the other side, each one used their magic to disappear. Little-paw went last. With a swish of her three tails, she vanished.

Poppy gave herself a shake. There was no time to stand here feeling sad; she needed to help Natasha.

She hurried back along the riverbank, hoping desperately that Sir Fitzroy hadn't caught her

friend. Shouting came from her right, followed by a loud splash.

"Natasha?" she whispered. "It's me, Poppy!"

"Over here!" Natasha's face poked out from behind a tree. "Careful the guards don't see you! Did you free the foxes?"

Poppy dodged behind the tree trunk. "Yes, they've escaped! What happened to the kite?"

"I brought it down when I decided to hide.

Sir Fitzroy's ordered his guards to search the bushes," Natasha told her. "I think he's suspicious about the dragon now. He knows he's been tricked!"

There was another loud splash.

"What's going on?" said Poppy. "I hope they're not hurting some poor ducks."

The girls crept out from their hiding place. Angry voices echoed up the riverbank.

"Well, clearly this was NOT the right direction!" Sir Fitzroy yelled. "Now I am COLD and WET!"

Poppy giggled, pointing. "I don't believe it! They've fallen in!"

Sir Fitzroy was standing up to his waist in water with his hands on his hips. Two of the guards were also in the river. One was trying to climb the slippery, muddy bank.

"I'm sorry, sir!" said a guard. "I didn't notice the water."

"You're SORRY!" Sir Fitzroy spluttered. "That doesn't make up for it. You were the one who led us this way. What am I supposed to do if the water makes my armor rusty?"

Two guards took hold of the knight's arms and tried to haul him up the muddy bank, but they lost their footing and all three collapsed into the water again.

Poppy giggled so hard her stomach felt fluttery. "Sir Fitzroy looks so funny when he's angry, like a bull that's ready to charge!"

Natasha grinned. "And the best thing is that while he's stuck in there the foxes are getting away!"

Chapter Nine

✳ ⁂ ✳

A Good Sign

Poppy worked extra hard the next day to make up for not selling many candles the day before. She sold eleven Blue Whispers, fourteen Golden

Sparkles and twenty of the elephant-shaped candles that her aunt had made. Everyone seemed to love them.

She sold out so quickly that she had to return to the workshop to pick up more. A box of gorgeous red-and-gold dragon candles stood by the door.

She picked one up, admiring the beautiful wings and tail. "I've never seen you make dragons before," she said to her aunt.

"I've never tried," her aunt replied. "But I dreamed about dragons last night and when I woke up I had to make them."

"They're lovely!" said Poppy.

The people of Penlee liked them too and they gathered round Poppy in the street to buy them. Poppy was so busy that she didn't have a rest till lunchtime. Sitting down on a bench at midday, she noticed that the sign on the church gate had changed since the day before.

The sign that read MAGICAL ANIMALS ARE DANGEROUS had gone. In its place was a new sign written in large red letters. Poppy read it and a smile spread across her face.

Magical animals are special and they are welcome in our town.
This sign was written by the people of Penlee.

Poppy hugged her basket, a lump in her throat. It wasn't just her—lots of people in the town cared about magical creatures!

"Hello, Poppy!" Mr. Lott came out of the bakery. "Have you sold many candles this morning?"

"Yes, lots!" Poppy started to say. She broke off as Sir Fitzroy marched up the street, his armor clanking.

The knight stopped next to the new sign and scowled. "What's this? Who took my sign away? And who wrote this other one?"

"It says who wrote it," said Mr. Lott mildly. "It's by the people of this town."

"This is outrageous!" shouted Sir Fitzroy. "This is treachery! The queen shall hear of this."

A crowd began to gather. Natasha came out of the shoemaker's shop. She smiled at Poppy. Sir Fitzroy's guards ran to his side and waited, as if uncertain what to do.

"Tell the queen then!" called Natasha. "We don't mind."

"I SHALL tell the queen," replied the knight.

"You're all disobeying her royal orders. I shall make sure I tell her all about it."

Mr. Lott folded his arms over his floury apron. "Good! When you do, make sure you say that we are loyal subjects, but we don't believe magical animals should be captured. Perhaps if she left her castle to meet some of the creatures, she would understand them better."

"Meet them!" echoed Sir Fitzroy in horror. The rest of his words were lost as the crowd gave Mr. Lott a round of applause.

Sir Fitzroy's face darkened like a rain cloud. He ripped the new sign off the gate, crumpled it up, and threw it on the ground. "Guards! Get the horses!" he snapped. "We're leaving this awful town right now."

The crowd began to scatter and Natasha came to sit on the bench beside Poppy. "I don't think anyone will miss him!" she said, glancing at Sir Fitzroy.

"I know I won't!" said Poppy. "I'll miss Little-paw though."

"But maybe we can visit her or look for new magical animals to make friends with," Natasha smiled. "I've heard that sky unicorns sometimes stop by the river to drink. Or if we walk a bit farther we can reach the Whispering Forest and meet a star wolf."

"That's a good idea!" said Poppy, cheering up. "Come on, I'll buy you a slice of cake."

The girls wandered into the bakery and gazed at the rows of delicious buns and cakes behind the counter.

"That chocolate cake with the swirly icing looks nice," said Natasha.

"Two slices of chocolate cake, please," Poppy told Mr. Lott.

The baker parceled their cake into white paper bags. "Here you are, Poppy. Have you got any new candles for sale?"

"Yes, my aunt made these dragon ones." Poppy picked one out of the basket to show him.

"Dragon candles! Your aunt has a good imagination. Look at those wonderful red wings." Mr. Lott turned the waxy dragon in his hand. "It's funny—Mr. Denton the shoemaker looked out of his window last night and he says he's sure he saw a dragon flying over the river. He could see its fiery breath."

"Really? You don't often see dragons round here." Natasha took a bite of her chocolate cake.

Mr. Lott looked closely at the girls. "I don't suppose you girls know anything about it, do you?"

"Um. . ." began Poppy.

"Well. . ." started Natasha.

"Actually, I don't think I really need to know." Mr. Lott winked at them. "Take care, girls. I must check on the bread in the oven." He went whistling into the back room.

Natasha took another bite of cake. "Thanks for the cake. It's really delicious!"

Poppy smiled. "I've got to go back to the workshop. Would you like to come with me and see how the candles are made?"

"Yes, please!" Natasha grinned back. "Especially the Red Flamers!"

Poppy linked arms with Natasha as they climbed the hill to her house. She felt so lucky to have a stone that let her talk to magical animals, and a friend to share adventures with!

Don't miss another secret rescue!
Can Emma help a star wolf cub
keep the stars shining?